BUMP SATURDAY

as told to Roger Hargreaves

A Thurman Book

PRICE/STERN/SLOAN
Publishers, Ltd., London

Hello! I'm Mr Bump.

And today is Saturday.

And what a day it's been!

Now, you know why I'm called Mr Bump, don't you?

It's because I keep on having little accidents.

But, they are not my fault.

Really!

They just happen!

Today especially!

It all started when I woke up this morning.

I opened an eye.

And then I opened the other eye.

And those were about the only things that went right today.

The sun was shining in through the bedroom window.

"What a lovely day," I thought.

And I jumped out of bed.

OUCH!

I had jumped out of bed on the wrong side, and hit the bedroom wall.

I went into the bathroom.

And tripped over the mat!

And fell into the bath!

"OUCH!" again.

I squeezed the toothpaste out of the tube on to my toothbrush.

Oh, dear.

And then I went downstairs.

Actually, I went downstairs much more quickly than usual.

BUMPBUMPBUMPBUMPBUMP!

"OUCH!" times five.

I went into the kitchen to make myself some breakfast.

I was going to have a boiled egg, marmalade on toast, and a cup of coffee.

What I actually had was boiled coffee, marmalade on floor, and a cup of egg!

I picked up the Saturday paper to read what had happened in the rest of the world.

I opened it.

And, somehow or other, it tore into two halves!

All by itself!

What a way to start the day!

Then I thought I would go for a walk.

A mistake.

I opened my front door.

So far, so good.

And then, I felt something in my hand.

What was it?

The door knob!

Oh, dear.

I stepped outside.

Mistake number two!

I tripped over the doorstep!

And staggered into an apple tree!

And trod on an apple!

And went head over heels into a prickly rose bush!

And jumped out!

And slipped on the grass!

And finished up in my hedge!

Half in, and half out!

A chapter of accidents!

I somehow managed to get myself out of the hedge, and off I went for my walk.

Mistake number three!

I saw Mr Silly, Mr Greedy and Mr Nosey playing football in the park.

"Hello," they shouted to me. "Come and play!"

I rushed up and took a kick at the ball.

A really big kick!

Mistake number four!

"OUCH!" shouted Mr Silly, as I kicked him on the shin.

I tried again.

"OUCH!" gasped Mr Greedy, holding his tummy!

One more try.

A really good try!

"OOOOOOO!" yelped Mr Nosey,
holding his nose!

Today has been a very long Saturday.

Here a BUMP!

There a BUMP!

Everywhere a BUMP BUMP!

I even managed to trip over poor little Mr Small!

A chapter of accidents!

After apologising to Mr Small, I thought I had better go home before anything else happened.

I couldn't open the door because it didn't have a door knob, so I had to climb in through the window.

By this time I had lost count of the mistakes I had made, but that was certainly one of them!

After I had swept up the broken flower pot, I thought I had better have supper and an early bedtime before anything else went wrong.

Cheese on toast seemed a good idea.

Well.

Actually.

It finished up as cheese on carpet!

And so to bed.

"It really has been one of those days," I thought to myself as I jumped into bed.

And landed in the bed.

The flowerbed!

Somehow or other I had jumped out of
the window!

So, here I am, sitting in a flowerbed, looking at the moon.

And thinking what a day today has turned out to be.

Just one accident after another!

A chapter of accidents!

Bump Saturday!

One of these days I'm going to write a
book about it!